Groundhog at Evergreen Road

Book layout: Marcin D. Pilchowski
Editor: Laura Gates Galvin
Editorial assistance: Chelsea Shriver

First Edition 2003
10 9 8 7 6 5 4 3 2 1
Printed in Singapore

Acknowledgments:
　　Our very special thanks to Dr. Don E. Wilson of the Department of Systematic Biology at the Smithsonian
Institution's National Museum of Natural History for his curatorial review.
　　Soundprints would also like to thank Ellen Nanney and Robyn Bissette at the Smithsonian Institution's
Office of Product Development and Licensing for their help in the creation of this book.
　　Soundprints would also like to acknowledge Shawn Gould for his valuable artistic contribution to this project.

Library of Congress Cataloging-in-Publication Data

Korman, Susan.
　　Groundhog at Evergreen Road / by Susan Korman ; illustrated by Higgins Bond.
　　　p. cm.
　　Summary: A young groundhog builds a burrow of his own for the first time in a backyard
that has plenty of food and other conveniences.
　　ISBN 1-59249-022-0 – ISBN 1-59249-023-9 (micro hbk.) – ISBN 1-59249-024-7 (pbk.)
　　　1. Woodchuck—Juvenile fiction. [1. Woodchuck—Fiction.] I. Bond, Higgins, ill. II. Title.

　　PZ10.3.K845 Gr 2003
　　[E]—dc21
　　　　　　　　　　　　　　　　　　　　　　　　　　　2002191155

Groundhog at Evergreen Road

by Susan Korman

Illustrated by Higgins Bond

Soundprints

Where Children Discover...

It is early morning and the sun is beginning to rise. Above the brick house on Evergreen Road, bright streaks of pink paint the sky. At the birdfeeder, two cardinals chatter back and forth.

It is still dark and cool when Groundhog wakes inside his burrow. His mother, three brothers and sister are already awake.

5

Ten weeks ago, when Groundhog was born, he weighed only an ounce. He had no fur and he couldn't open his eyes.

Now Groundhog weighs almost four pounds! His coat is grayish brown, with a bit of red on his belly. His legs and bushy tail are black.

Groundhog blinks as he follows his mother into the bright sunshine. During the first six weeks of his life, Groundhog drank only his mother's milk. Now he eats clover, alfalfa and other tender grasses on his own.

Groundhog hurries past his family in search of his morning meal. He makes his way across the wide lawn behind the brick house. Soon Groundhog spots a new treat in the vegetable garden—ripe green beans!

Groundhog creeps closer to the vegetable garden. As he eats the delicious green beans, he stops to look around every few minutes. With his sharp eyes, he checks to make sure that no predators lurk nearby. The red fox, hawk and coyote are especially dangerous to Groundhog. *Bang!* A sudden noise pierces the quiet morning.

The back door of the brick house
opens and a large dog lumbers outside. Her metal
tags clink together as she trots toward the vegetable garden—and Groundhog!
Groundhog rises on his haunches. The dog sniffs the ground and the air, then
spots Groundhog. She barks twice and bounds toward him.

13

Groundhog immediately lets out a loud, shrill sound. The dog freezes, startled. Groundhog whistles again.

This time Groundhog's defense does the trick. The frightened dog whirls around and races back toward the house.

Once the dog is safely inside, Groundhog begins to eat again. When he is finally full, he waddles toward the burrow. But Groundhog is not returning home to his mother. It is time for him to dig his own den.

Groundhog finds the right spot for his burrow at the edge of the yard. He uses the claws on his front paws to dig and the claws on his back paws to kick the loose dirt away. Soon he reaches a thick tree root. He gnaws through the root with his four sharp incisor teeth, and continues tunneling downward.

Groundhog's new home will be more than a simple tunnel. When he has dug about six feet underground, he begins to carve out a sleeping chamber. He carefully lines it with dry leaves. Next to his "bedroom," he digs a special toilet room.

Now Groundhog begins to work on another entrance to his tunnel. This will be a secret escape route!

Groundhog's escape route, or "plunge hole," heads straight down into his den, giving Groundhog a way of quickly escaping from his enemies.

It is late afternoon when Groundhog finishes digging. He is tired—and ready to eat again.

Slowly, Groundhog makes his way back toward the brick house. This time he finds clover and dandelion greens in the yard. On the way back to his den, Groundhog spots a pile of smooth rocks. Lazily, he stretches out on the cool rocks to rest.

A loud whistle suddenly rings through the air! Within a second, Groundhog is up on his hind feet again. He recognizes his mother's cry—a sign that danger is near!

A moment later, Groundhog spots the threat. Just above the treetops is a hawk. Her wide wings extended, she dips and swoops, searching the ground below for a meal.

Luckily, Groundhog isn't far from his burrow. He darts toward his plunge hole. By the time his mother whistles again, he is safely hidden below ground.

By now, dusk is beginning to fall on Evergreen Road. As the sun sinks below the treetops, Groundhog pokes his head out of his burrow to make sure that the threat is gone. The early evening air is still and quiet. The hawk is gone. Groundhog is safe. Back in his cozy burrow, he is soon fast asleep.

About the Groundhog

The groundhog is found in Canada and Alaska, as well as in the northern regions of the eastern and central United States. The groundhog is a marmot, a type of ground-dwelling squirrel related to chipmunks and prairie dogs. Other names for the groundhog include "woodchuck" and "whistle-pig," because of the high-pitched whistle it makes when frightened.

Groundhogs grow to about 20-27 inches long and weigh between 5-10 pounds. They are heaviest in late fall, right before their hibernation begins. They feed mainly on grasses, alfalfa and clover.

Throughout North America, February 2nd is celebrated as "Groundhog Day." On this day, groundhogs supposedly emerge from hibernation to predict whether spring will be coming soon. This tradition began with European farmers, who had similar traditions with badgers, bears and other animals. While people enjoy believing in this legend, the groundhog is not an accurate predictor of weather.

Glossary

burrow: A hole or den in the ground that an animal digs to use as a home.

defense: A behavior used by an animal to protect itself.

hibernation: A state of deep sleep in which some animals pass the winter.

hind: Back or rear.

incisor: A cutting front tooth in mammals.

marmot: A burrowing rodent.

plunge hole: A vertical entrance to a burrow used by groundhogs to escape danger.

predator: An animal that hunts and eats other animals.

Points of Interest in This Book